[redacted]

Dear Parent:

Congratulations! Your child is taking the first steps on an exciting journey. The destination? Independent reading!

STEP INTO READING® will help your child get there. The program offers five steps to reading success. Each step includes fun stories and colorful art. There are also Step into Reading Sticker Books, Step into Reading Math Readers, Step into Reading Phonics Readers, Step into Reading Write-In Readers, and Step into Reading Phonics Boxed Sets—a complete literacy program with something to interest every child.

Learning to Read, Step by Step!

Ready to Read   Preschool–Kindergarten
• big type and easy words • rhyme and rhythm • picture clues
For children who know the alphabet and are eager to begin reading.

Reading with Help   Preschool–Grade 1
• basic vocabulary • short sentences • simple stories
For children who recognize familiar words and sound out new words with help.

Reading on Your Own   Grades 1–3
• engaging characters • easy-to-follow plots • popular topics
For children who are ready to read on their own.

Reading Paragraphs   Grades 2–3
• challenging vocabulary • short paragraphs • exciting stories
For newly independent readers who read simple sentences with confidence.

Ready for Chapters   Grades 2–4
• chapters • longer paragraphs • full-color art
For children who want to take the plunge into chapter books but still like colorful pictures.

STEP INTO READING® is designed to give every child a successful reading experience. The grade levels are only guides. Children can progress through the steps at their own speed, developing confidence in their reading, no matter what their grade.

Remember, a lifetime love of reading starts with a single step!

TM & © 2012 Marvel & Subs. All rights reserved. Published in the United States by Random House Children's Books, a division of Random House, Inc., 1745 Broadway, New York, NY 10019, and in Canada by Random House of Canada Limited, Toronto.

Step into Reading, Random House, and the Random House colophon are registered trademarks of Random House, Inc.

Visit us on the Web!
StepIntoReading.com
randomhouse.com/kids
www.marvel.com

Educators and librarians, for a variety of teaching tools, visit us at randomhouse.com/teachers

ISBN: 978-0-307-93019-4 (trade) — ISBN: 978-0-375-97021-4 (lib. bdg.)

Printed in the United States of America
10 9 8 7 6 5 4 3 2 1

STEP INTO READING®

STEP 3

IRON MAN™
ARMORED ADVENTURES
THE MIGHT OF DOOM

Adapted by Dennis R. Shealy

Based on the episode
"Might of Doom" by Brandon Auman

Illustrated by Patrick Spaziante

Random House 🏠 New York

Teenager Tony Stark
and his friends Rhodey and Pepper
are in class.
Their teacher tells them
about a country called Latveria.

Latveria is ruled
by an evil armored villain.
His name is Doctor Doom!

Tony is really the hero
known as Iron Man!
He and his friends
race back to his secret armory.
They want to learn more
about Doctor Doom.

Iron Man's enemy, Obadiah Stane,
meets secretly with Doctor Doom.
Stane gives him the stolen plans
for Iron Man's armor.

In the armory,
Tony and his friends
discover the theft.

"I am going to get the stolen plans back," Tony says.

Pepper finds out more about Doom.

He was once a young genius,

just like Tony!

But Doom was injured

in a terrible accident.

Doom locked himself
into his mighty armor.
He became evil and
hungry for power.
"Tony, be careful,"
says Pepper.

Doom agrees to help Stane
with his secret project.
It is called the Monger Core.
"I will make it smaller
and more powerful,"
says Doom.

Suddenly, Doom's sensors detect something— Iron Man!

Outside the lab,
Iron Man uses his stealth
armor to spy on Stane.
He does not think
he will be discovered.

The armory's computer flashes.

Over the comm-link,

Rhodey warns Iron Man

that something is sneaking

up on him.

Doctor Doom surprises
Iron Man!

Doom powers up his armor!

It crackles with energy.

Doom blasts Iron Man
with his powerful
energy bolts.

18

He sends Iron Man
crashing through
a skyscraper!

19

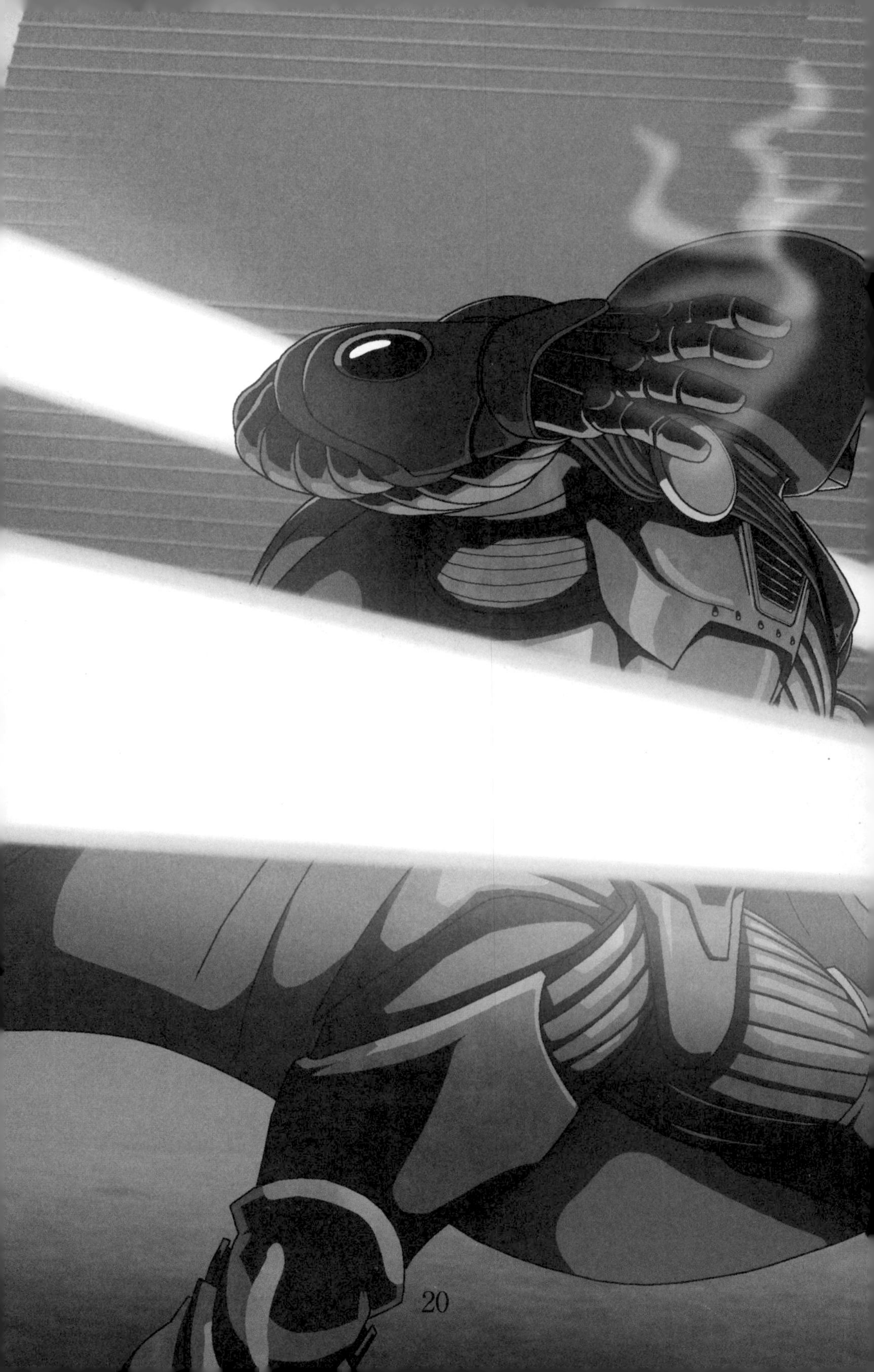

Iron Man fires back.

His blasts do not

stop Doctor Doom!

Doom creates
a storm of energy.
He throws
Iron Man into it.
The energy begins to tear
Iron Man's armor apart.

Rhodey arrives
in the War Machine armor
to help Iron Man.

War Machine and Iron Man

fire at Doom.

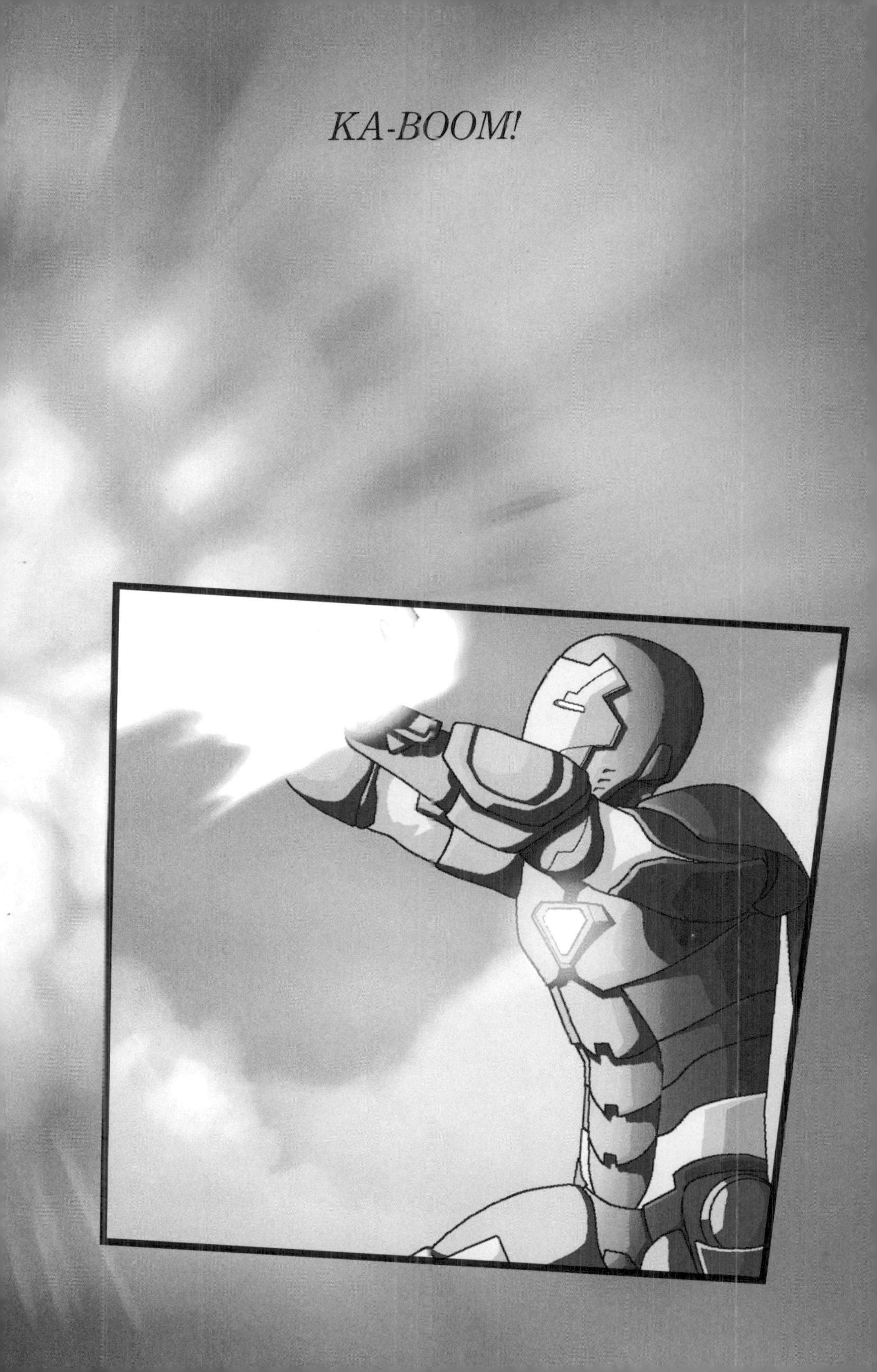
KA-BOOM!

Doom rises.

He is unharmed!

Doctor Doom attacks
Iron Man and
War Machine again!

Tony scans Doom's armor.

The heroes take off.

They will form a new plan.

Tony examines the scans
he took of Doom's armor.
Tony will find a way to stop him.

Doom and Stane meet
at the Stark Building.
Doom has made
the Monger Core
smaller and more
powerful.

He leaves with the
Iron Man armor plans.
Doom's business with Stane
is done.

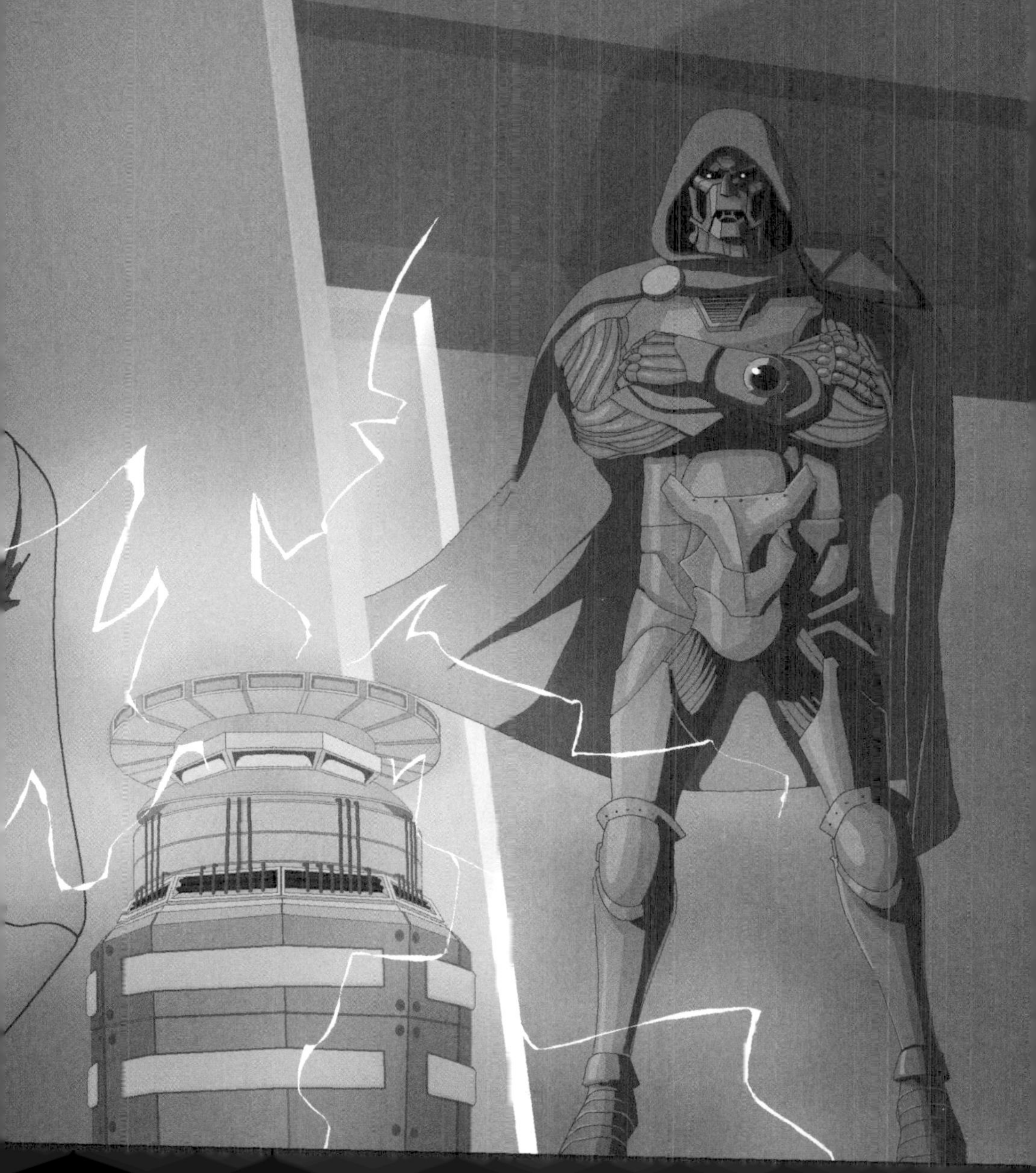

But the core
begins to glow.
It is using too much power.
Doom has tricked Stane!

Iron Man tracks

the Monger Core's energy signal.

The Monger Core has turned

the Stark Building into a giant bomb!

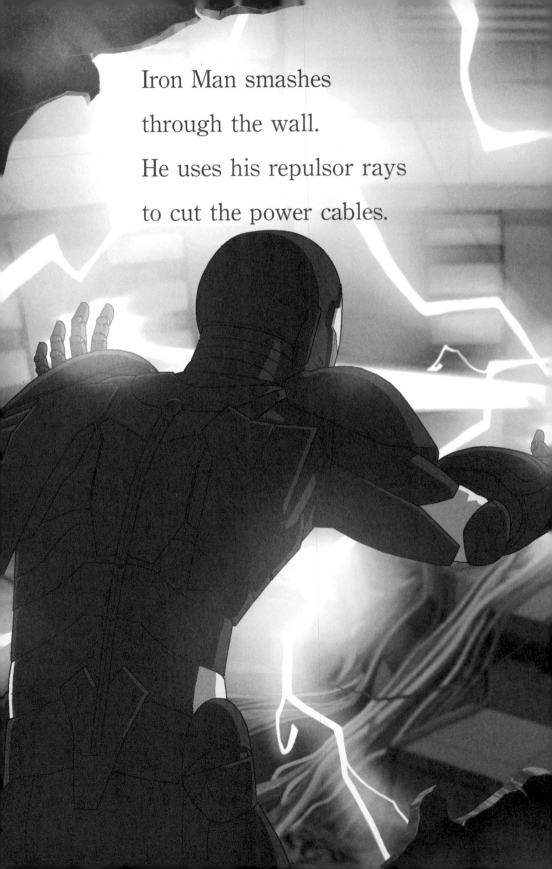

Iron Man smashes
through the wall.
He uses his repulsor rays
to cut the power cables.

It is too late!

The Monger Core

is going to explode!

Stane runs away.

Iron Man uses
his force field.
Will it be enough to contain
the Monger Core's energy?

"Yes!" Pepper cheers.

Iron Man has stopped

the explosion!

But Stane has escaped.

Doctor Doom flies away
in his jet.
He is angry—
the Monger Core
did not explode.

Iron Man stops Doom's jet.

He will not let Doom get away.

Iron Man and War Machine

blast Doom.

Doom creates

an energy storm

that is bigger than before!

The heroes
cannot reach him.

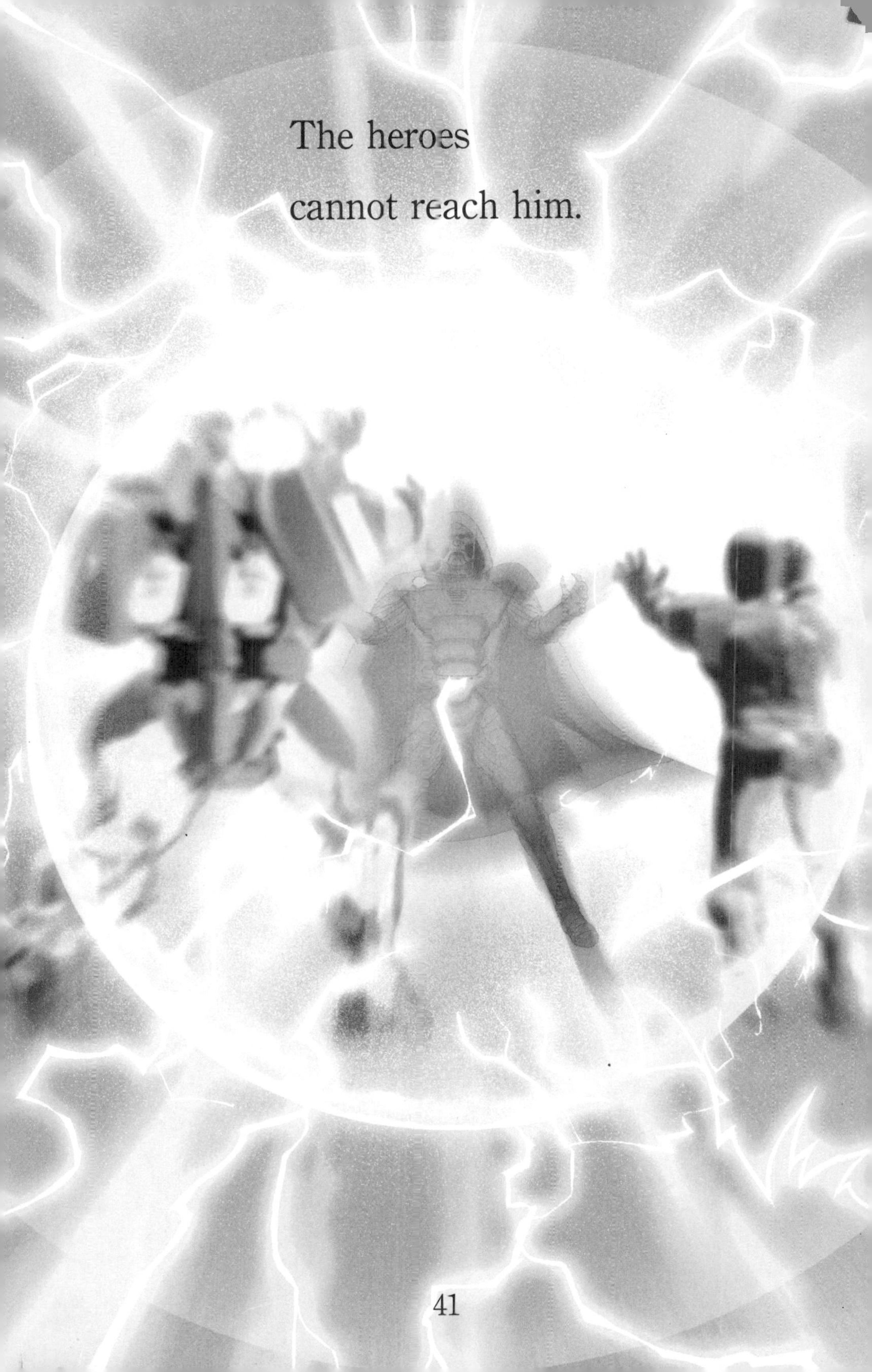

"Now you will feel
the might of Doom!"
the villain roars.
Suddenly,
an airship arrives!

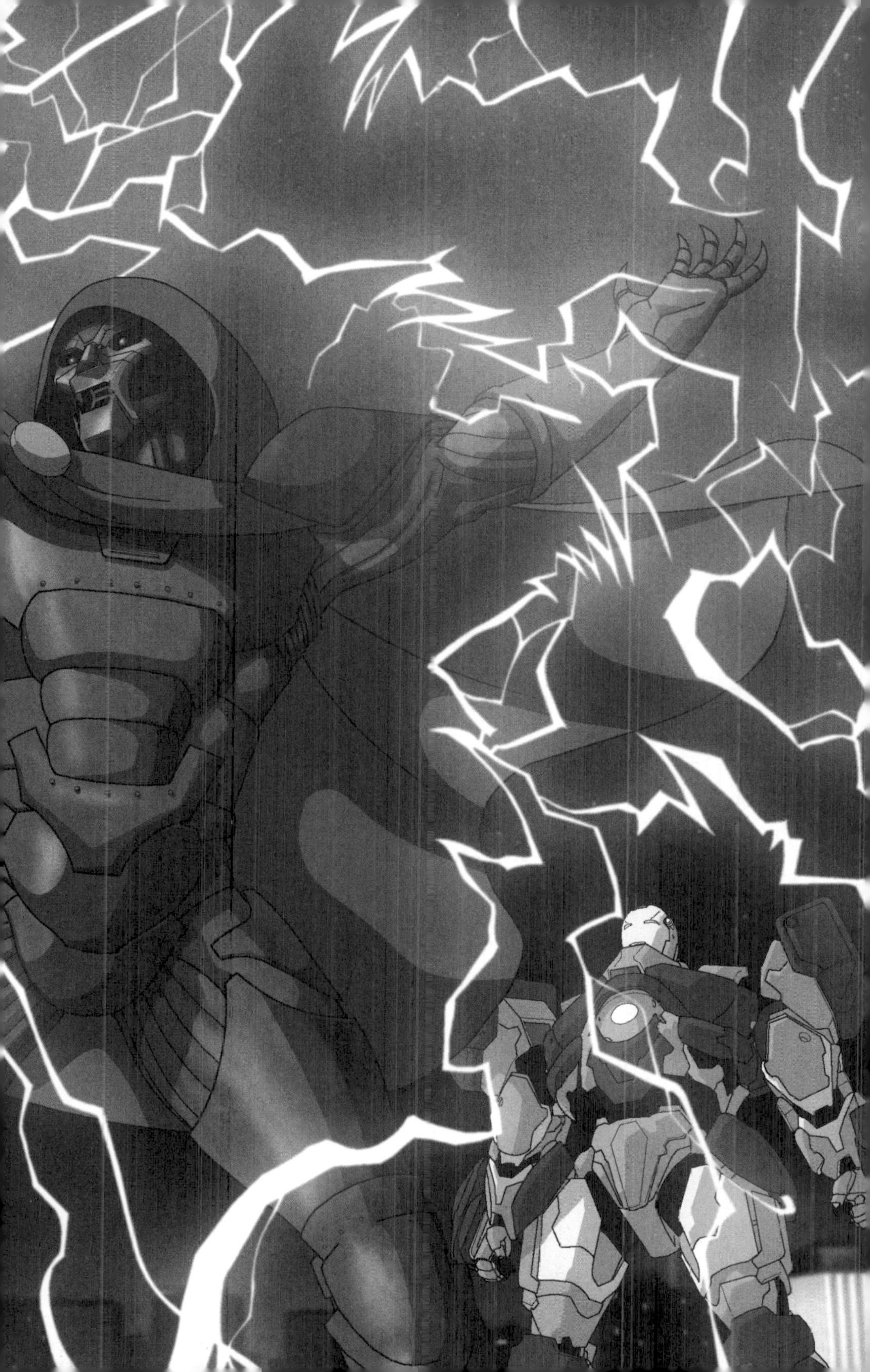

It is a Helicarrier for S.H.I.E.L.D.,
a high-tech police force
led by Nick Fury.
He orders them to stop fighting.

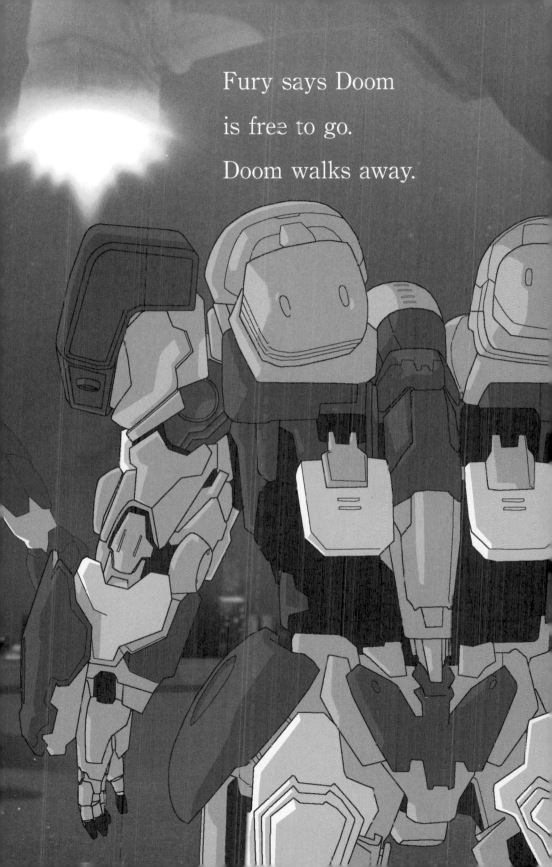

Fury says Doom
is free to go.
Doom walks away.

Iron Man tells Fury
about the bomb.

Fury asks Iron Man

for proof, but

Iron Man has none.

The proof was destroyed

when Iron Man stopped

the Monger Core from exploding.

Back in the armory,
Tony studies
Doom's armor.
He vows to one day bring
the villain to justice.